Pam Has a Map

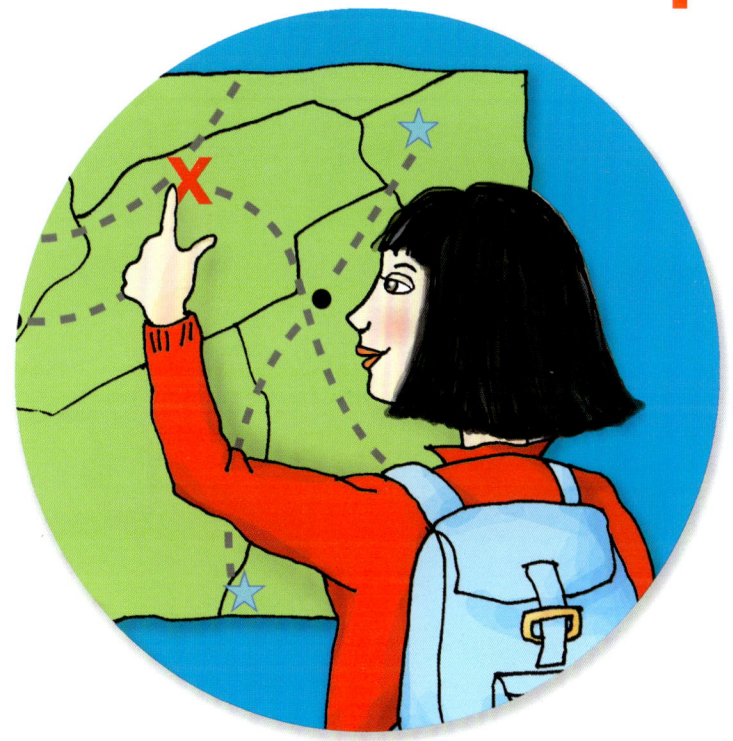

by Susan Hartley • illustrated by Anita DuFalla

Pam is fit.
Tam is fit.

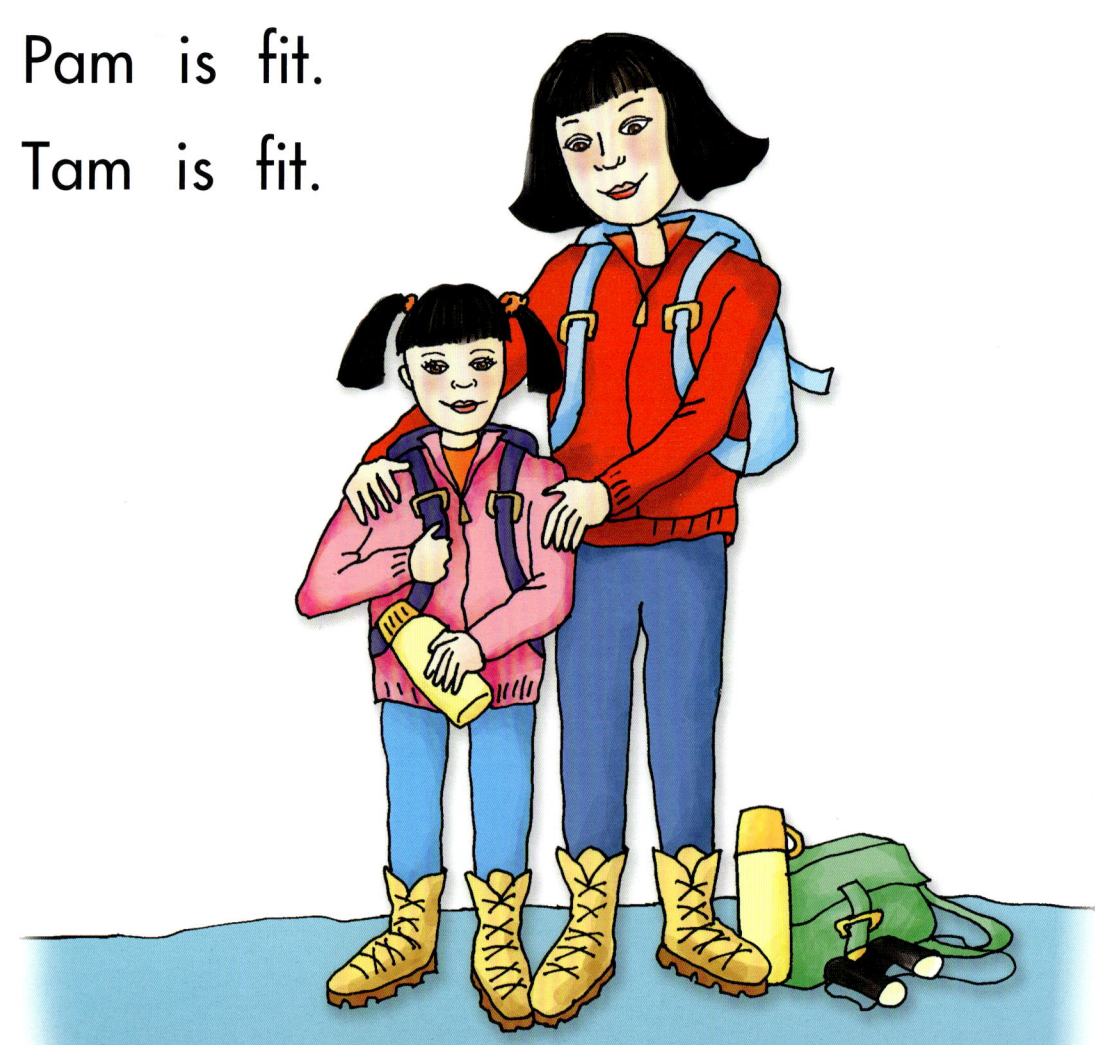

Pam has a map.

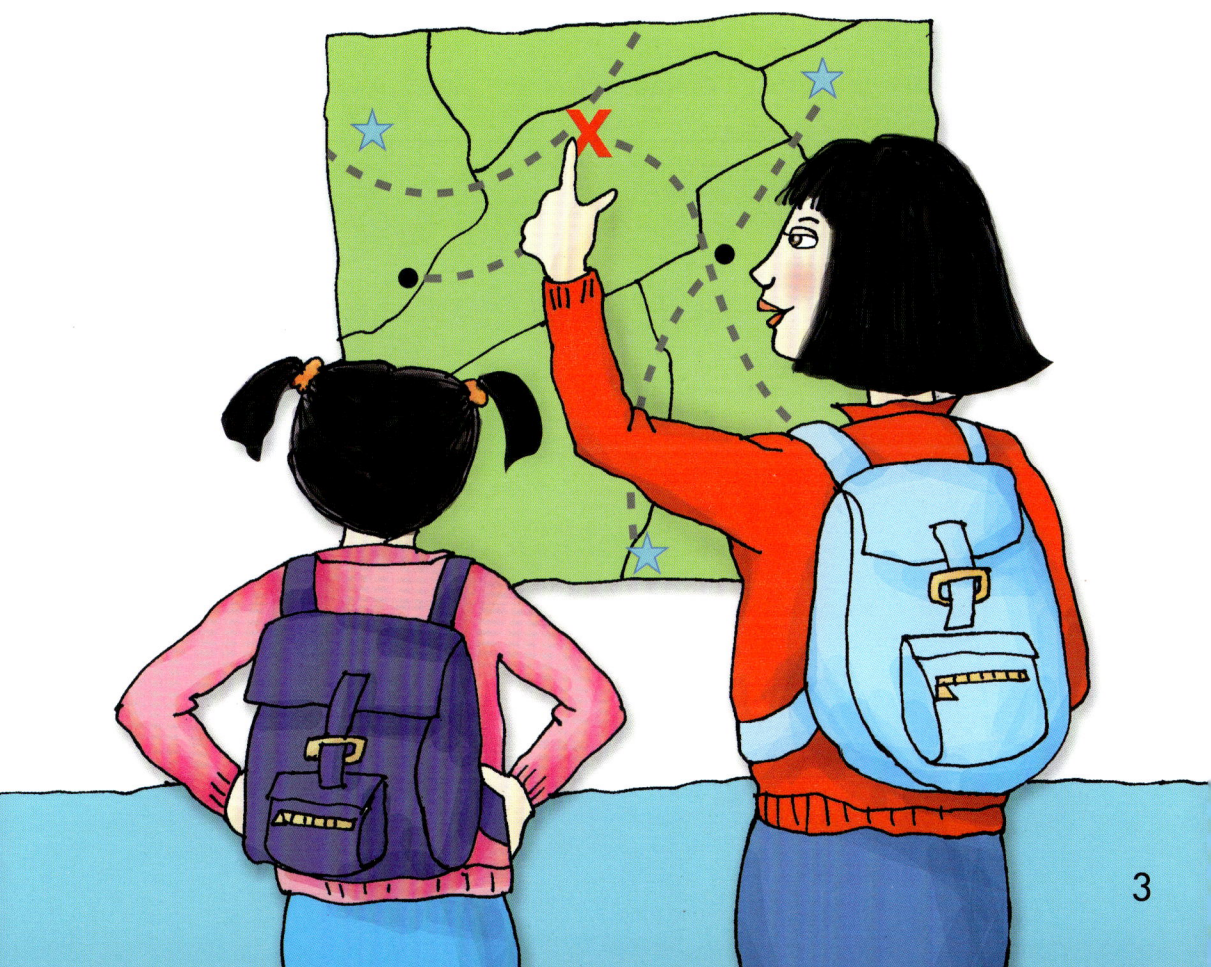

Pam has a pin.

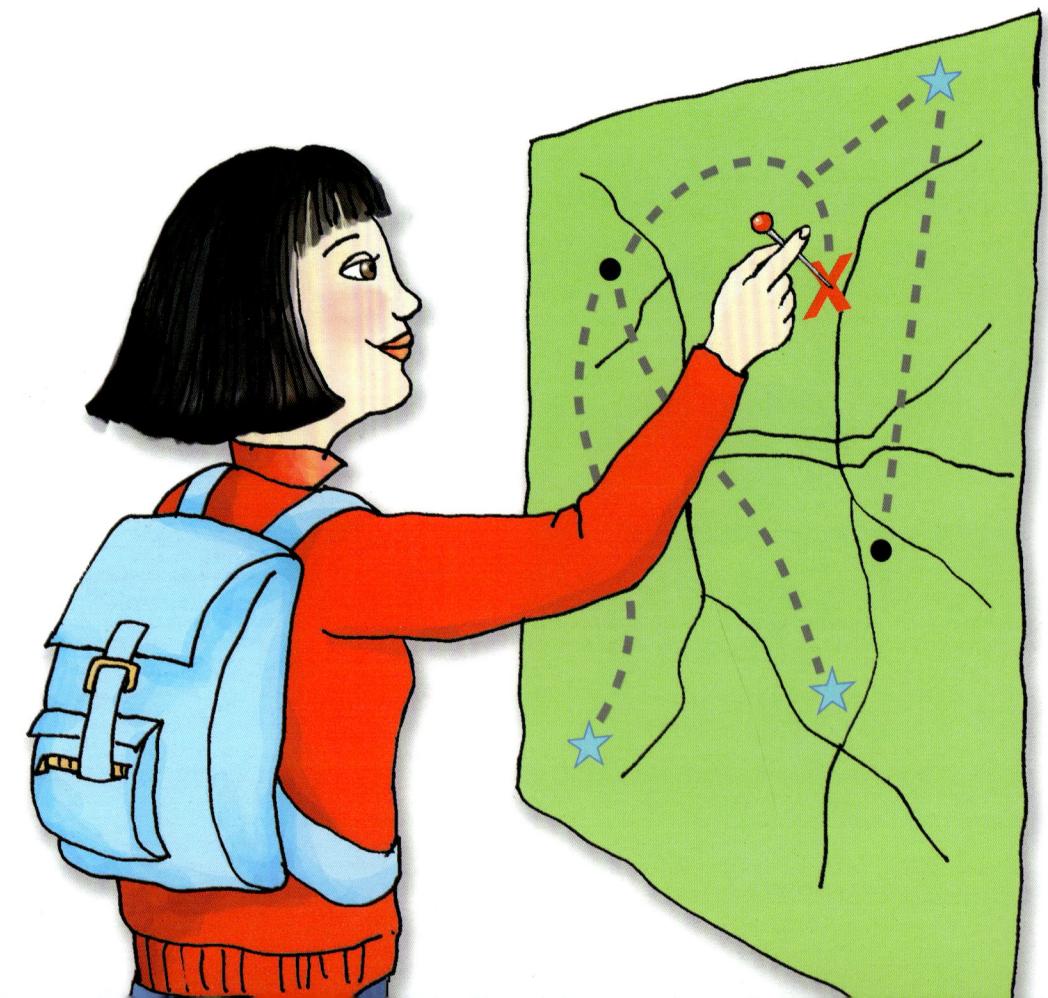

Pam sat.

Tam sat.

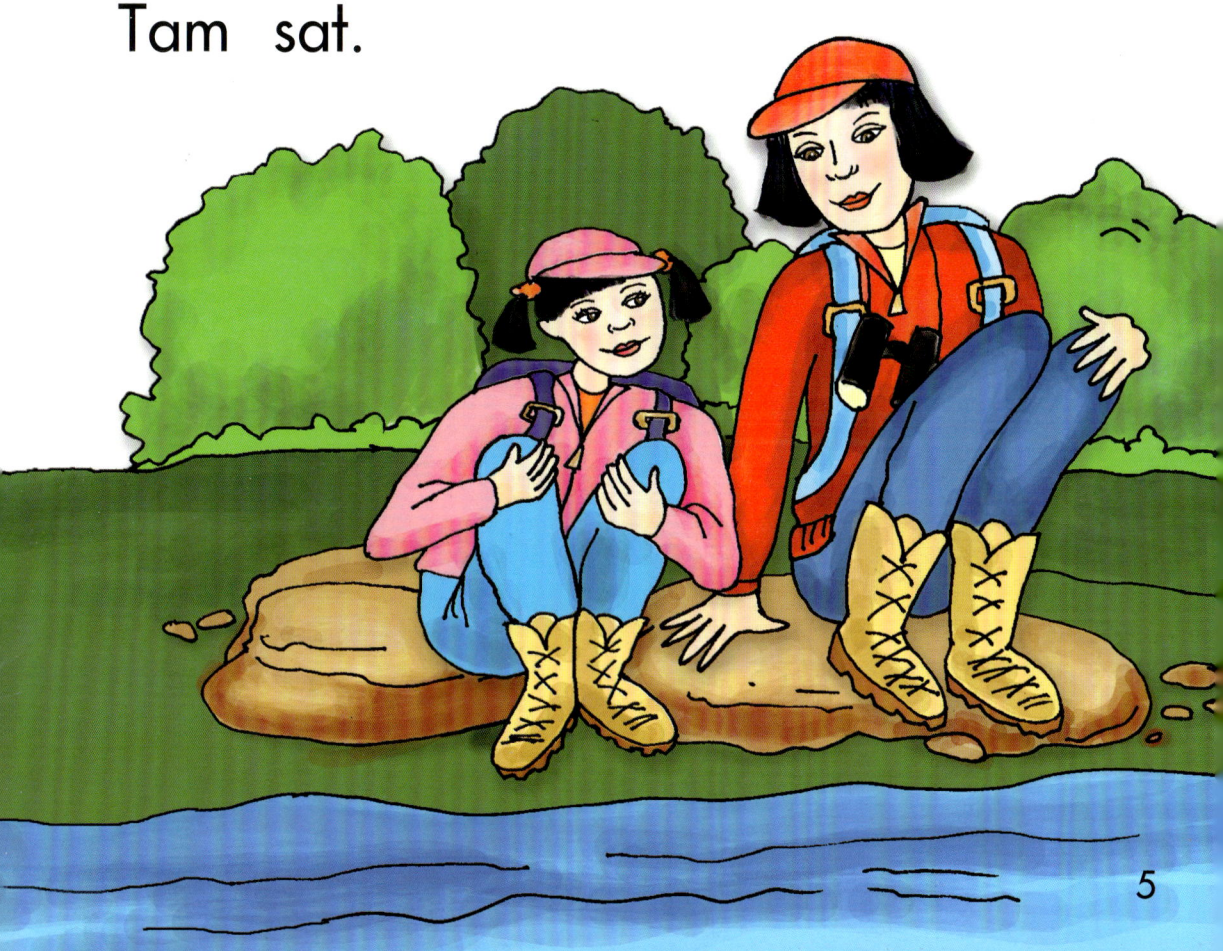

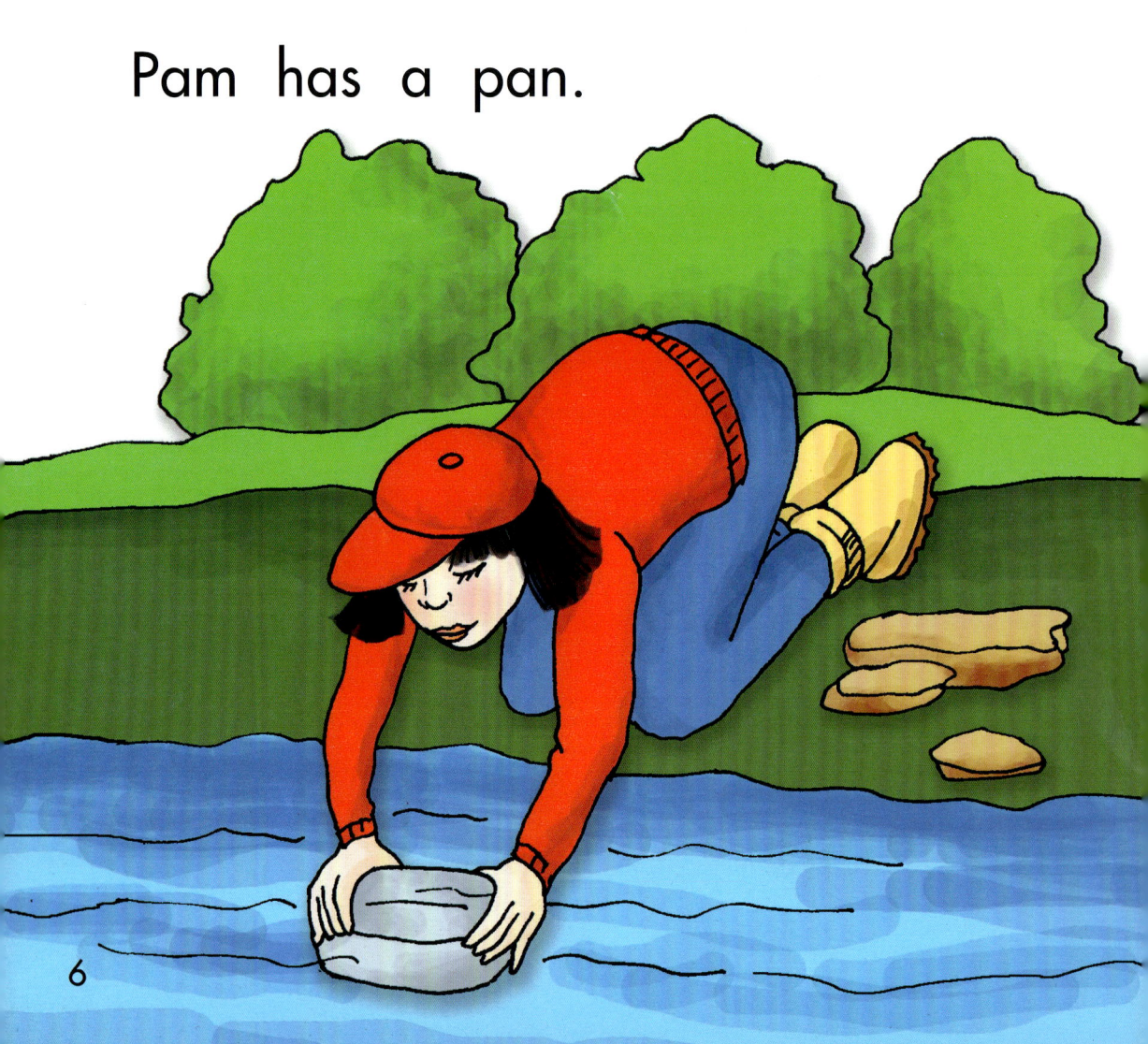

Pam has a sip.
Tam has a sip.

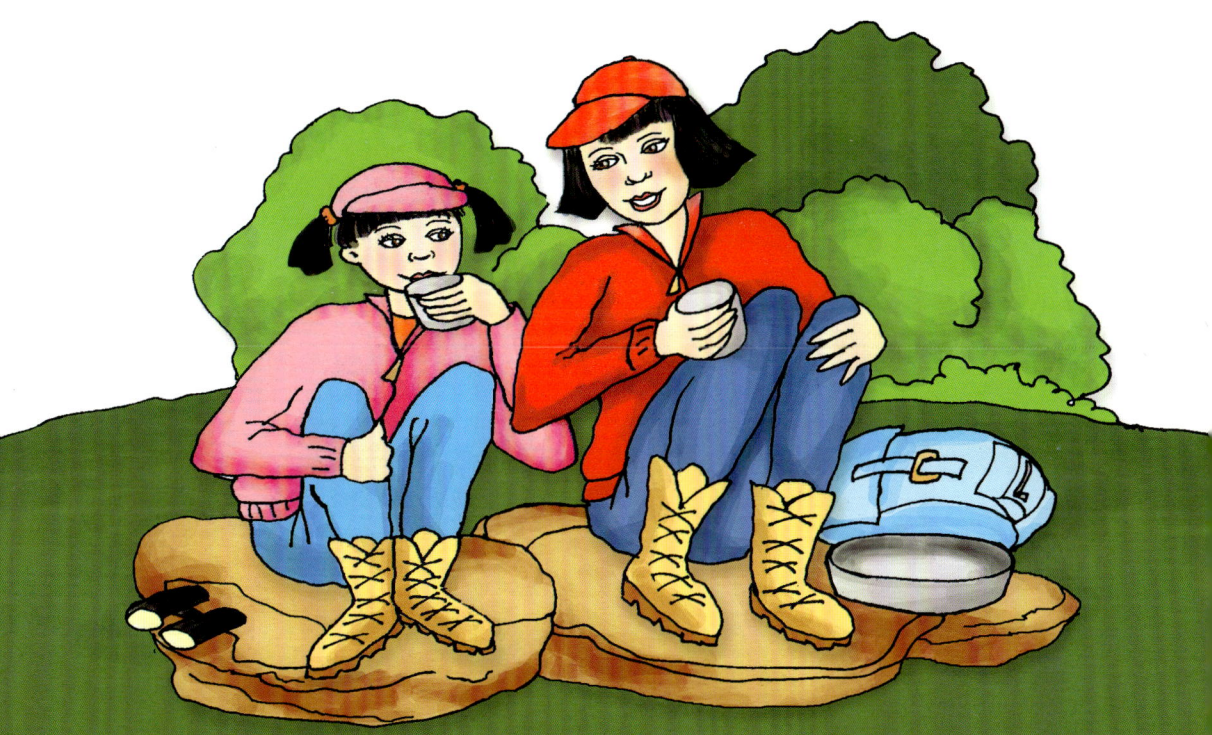

Tam has a nap.
Pam has a nap.

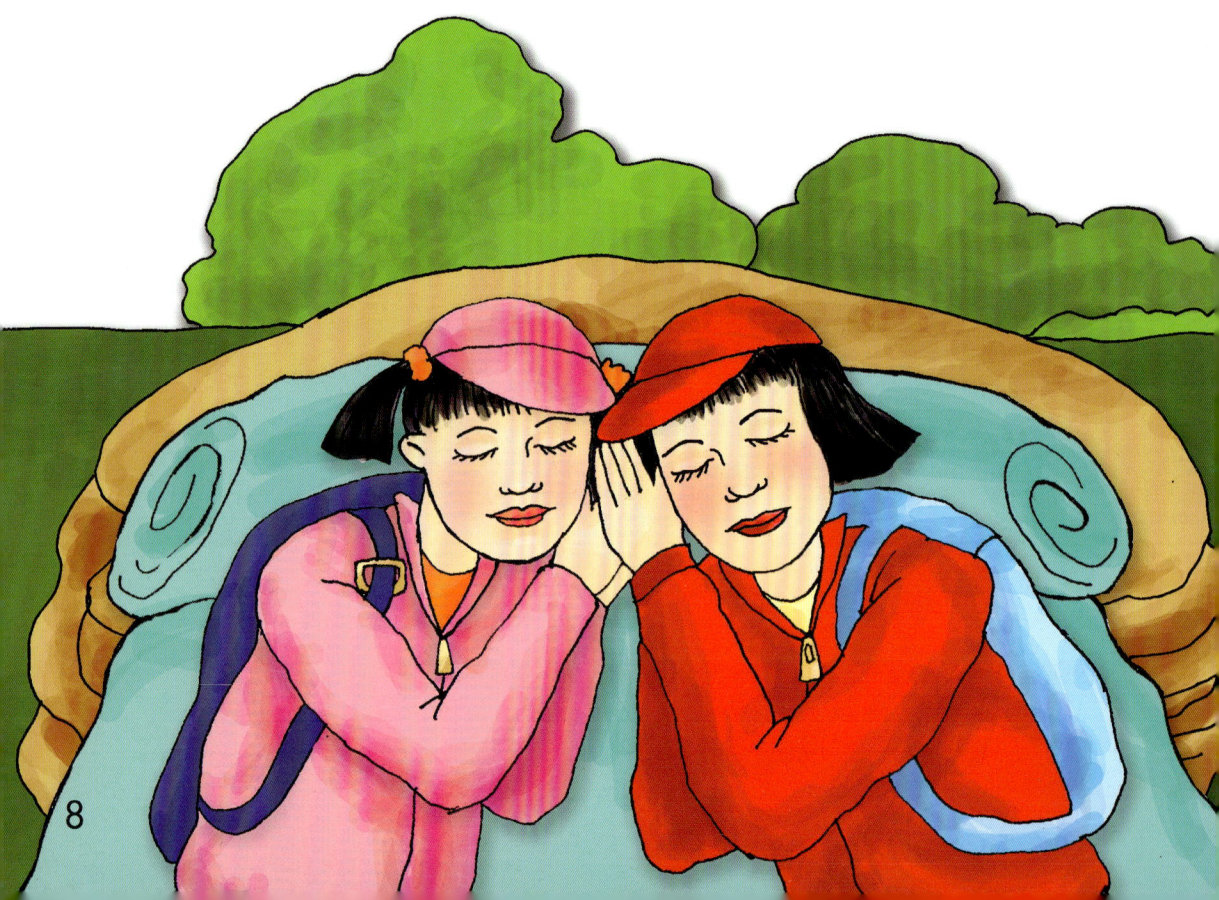